W9-CHA-352

DEDICATION
Aloha pumehana Beth & Teresa and the Keiki of Le Jardin Academy

— D.S.S.

THE GECKO WHO WANTED TO BE DIFFERENT
Written by Dorothy Sarna Saurer
Illustrated by Carole Hinds McCarty

Produced and published by

ISLAND HERITAGE
PUBLISHING
A DIVISION OF THE MADDEN CORPORATION
99-880 Iwaena Street
Aiea, Hawaii 96701-3202
(808) 487-7299
(808) 488-2279 (fax)
E-mail: hawaii4u@pixi.com

Printed in Hong Kong.

ISBN 0-89610-284-X

First edition, fourth printing, 1999

Written by Dorothy Sarna Saurer
Illustrated by Carole Hinds McCarty

Kupu the Gecko was feeling so sad!
And oh, great geckos! The problem he had!
He had a great body, so long and thin,
BUT – He didn't like the *color* of his *skin!*

First Kupu would moan and then he would groan,
And then he would say in the saddest tone,
"What color are geckos? We're not on the chart!
We're all gecko colored – can't tell us apart!
Oh, gecko-color is no color at all –
We just seem to blend in with every wall.
Hawaii is so beautiful and bright –
But WE look like we should hide day and night!
Gecko color," he'd moan, "is so yucky...
How did other critters get so lucky?

Why couldn't I have been a goldfish so bright
Or a zebra, who's striped like day and night.
Cats are many colors, and so are dogs,
And oh! the beautiful *green* skin of frogs!
Or the sunshiny yellow of a baby duck..
And chameleons CHANGE colors! Talk about luck!
Looking like everyone else makes me mad!
Why couldn't I have been checkered or plaid?

A parrot has more color than he could need.
Why, for half his color, I'd beg and plead.
Leopards stand out because of their spots –
I wish they'd share them – they have LOTS.
Every other gecko looks like my twin –
Oh, how I wish I had different skin!

Butterflies come in every beautiful shade
And horses, so handsome, lead a parade.
There's majestic colors on an eagle,
And peacocks are iridescent and regal.
Penguins, in tuxes, look always dressed up.
And what cute spots on a dalmatian pup!
Bumble bees look bright in yellow and black –
Geckos look like they're wearing a sack!

Pandas have black and white arranged just so,
And fireflies can light up and GLOW!
Some fish have different colors on each fin,
Oh, how I wish I could change my skin!

I wish I could have somehow gotten linked
With colors from dinosaurs, now extinct!
Then there's the neat colors of a giraffe-
With so much skin, he could give geckos half!
Lions are all kings with their golden manes,
While geckos all look like just plain Jane's!
Our color belongs in the garbage bin –
Oh, how I wish I could change my skin!

I could be striped, rainbow-colored or dotted,
THEN for sure I'd be easily spotted!

Why am I just a plain colored lizard –
Oh, how I wish I could meet a wizard!
Who would snap her fingers and then – BEHOLD!
My skin would turn colors – maybe GOLD!"

Thinking about it, he danced and twirled –
"I'd be known as Gold Gecko around the world!
I'd be so famous with my skin of gold –
For me a red carpet would be rolled!"

Soon it was all Kupu could think about.
He'd HAVE to have gold skin, there was no doubt.

His teacher saw him dreaming and would scold,
"Kupu, stop dwelling on turning gold."
He felt like a loser, but knew he could win
If he could just change the color of his skin.
"I want to look different, shiny and bold,
And Wow! I'd look that way if I were gold!"

He lost his friends, who found him boring,
"It's worse," said one, "than my sister's snoring!"
They all considered his dream a big sin,
Geckos should be happy with gecko skin!

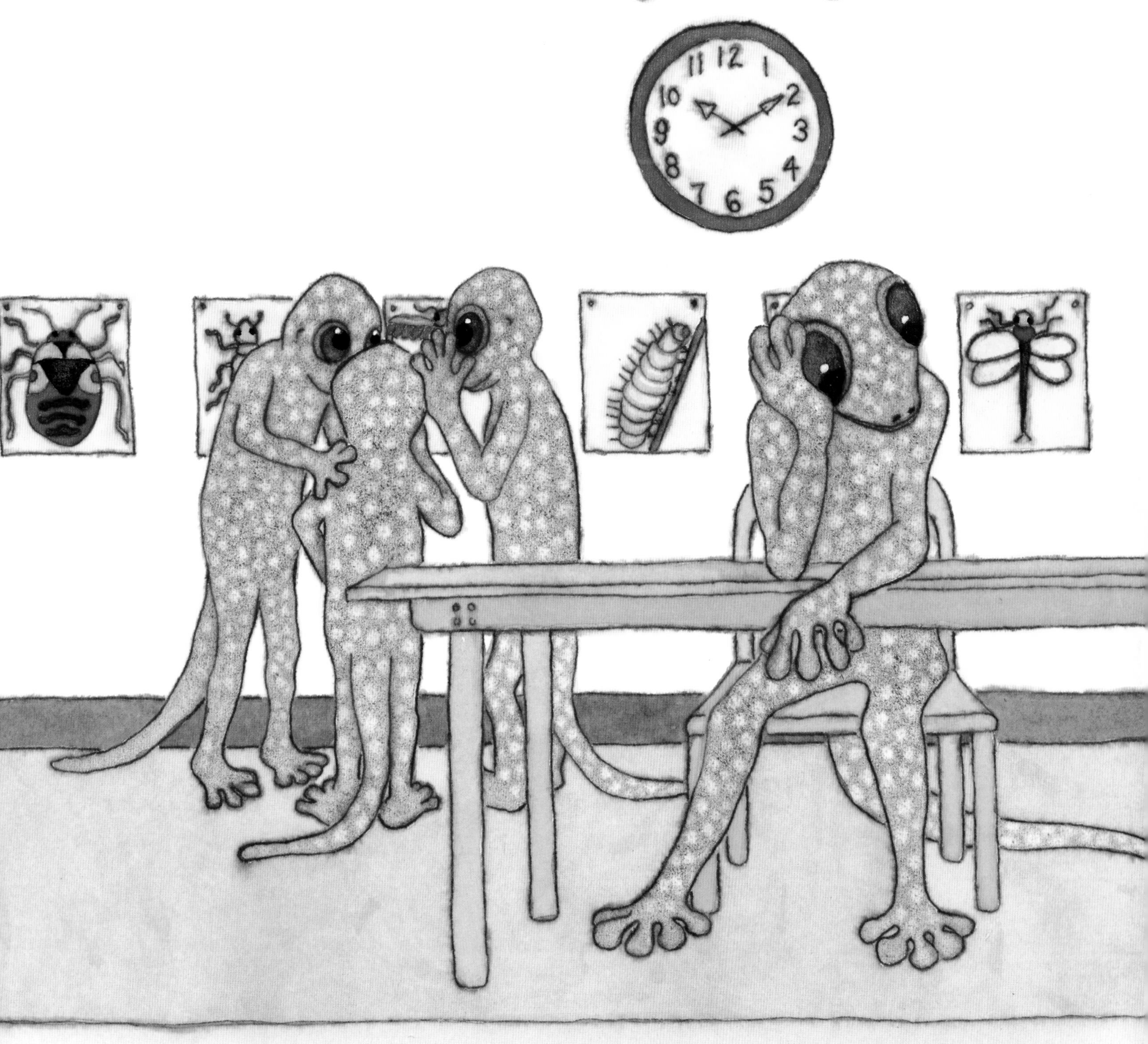
AaBbCcDdEeFfGgHhIiJjKkLlMm

But Kupu would moan and then he would groan,
And then he would say in a hopeful tone –
"I'd be a gecko that all would behold
If I could just have my skin turned gold...
Humans dye hair – I could dye my skin.
I'd DO it, but don't know how to begin...
TV talk shows don't have problems like THIS.
My problem makes all theirs seem like bliss.
Gecko color is uglier than MOLD!
Oh, how I wish my skin color were gold!"

One day when his mood was especially grim,
His father decided to talk to him.
"Kupu," he said, "Why complain and fuss?
You're acting like you're ashamed of us."

"Oh, no!" said Kupu, who loved his Mom and Dad,
"You're the BEST parents any gecko ever had!
It's just that every gecko looks like my twin,
I'd be different if I could change my skin!
Why do we all look alike?" he'd moan,
"I want to look LIKE JUST ME ALONE!
If I look in a mirror, I don't know
If I'm seeing me – or Lei, Kai or Joe!"

And poor Kupu looked so sad and blue,
His father said, “Here’s what we can do.
We can’t change the color of your skin,
But you CAN stop looking like everyone’s twin.”

“HOW?” Kupu asked, knowing his Dad was smart,
“I want to be different with all my heart.”

His Dad smiled and said, “Tomorrow you’ll see...
I’ll bring something for you home with me.
But in the meantime, you should think quite a bit
About being different and the meaning of it...
There’s a story about a sheep who was black
And every white sheep would turn its back
On the black sheep, because, right or wrong,
They felt the black sheep DIDN’T BELONG.
And the black sheep spent its days all alone,
“I wish I were like the others,” he’d moan.

Then his father said, with a special smile,
“Gecko color is always in style.
And we’re each special, though we look the same,
And no other gecko here has your NAME!”

Kupu thought hard ‘bout what his father said,
And many thoughts got mixed up in his head.
“...Maybe my skin color isn’t so bad...
After all, I look exactly like Dad
And he’s always special, without fail,
From the top of his head to the end of his tail.”

"I miss all my friends and want to play!
I can be *different* in another way...
I'll be the first gecko MOVIE STAR!
That's a good dream and I can go far!"

So, with a smile, Kupu fell asleep
And soon was counting look-alike sheep....

The next day he waited for his Dad,
And when he came home, was Kupu glad!

"Dad!" he exclaimed, with widening eyes,
"What's in the box? Oh! What's the surprise?"
He tore open the box, ripping the bow,
And seeing inside, gasped a big "OHHH!"

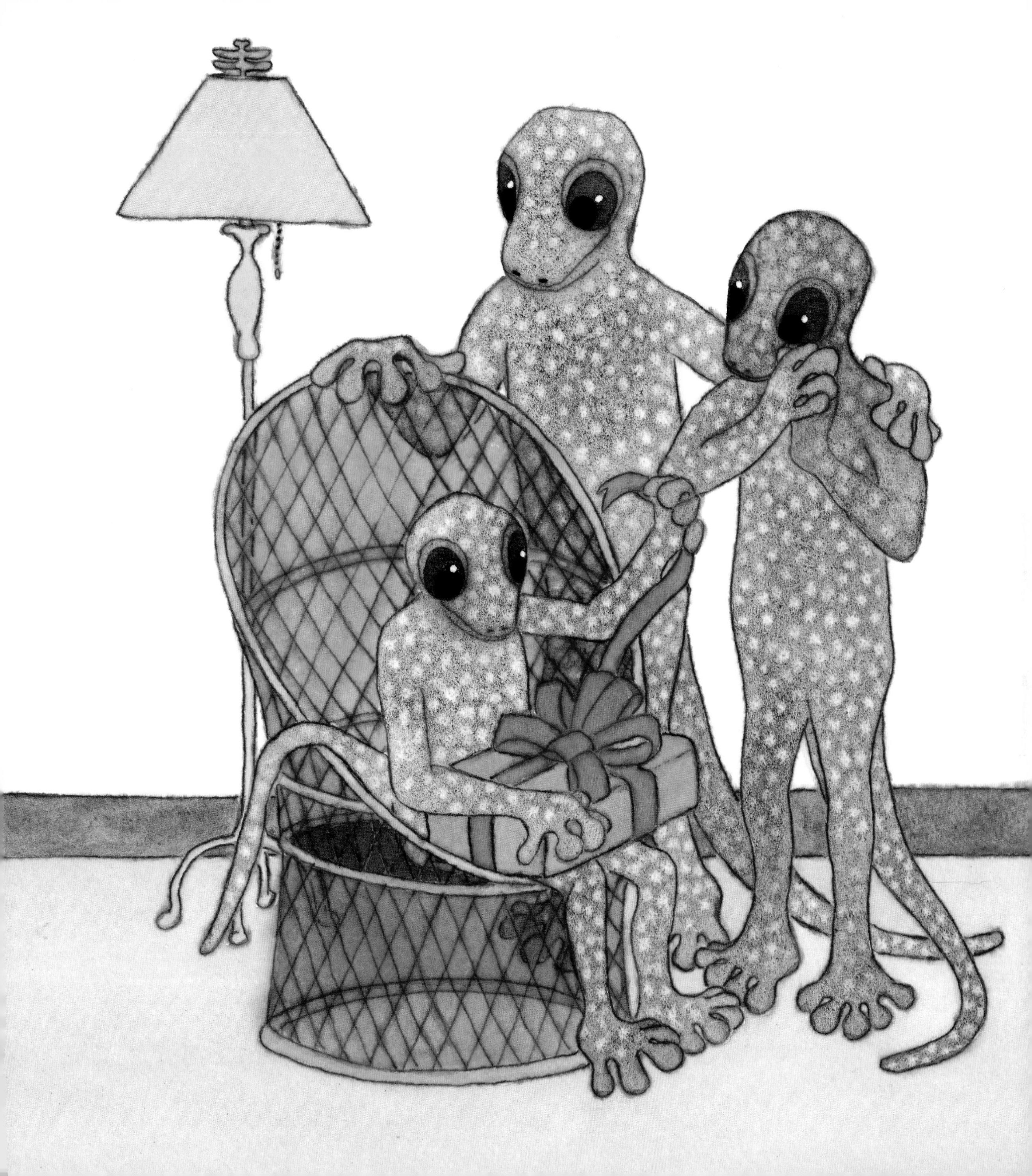

It was a T-shirt, but not the same
As others, for it had "KUPU," his name
In big red letters to cover his chest!
"Wow, Dad!" he said, "This will work the best!"
He put on the T-shirt with a big grin,
No longer concerned about his skin.
Kupu was happy as he could be –
"NOW EVERYONE KNOWS I AM REALLY ME!"

KUPU

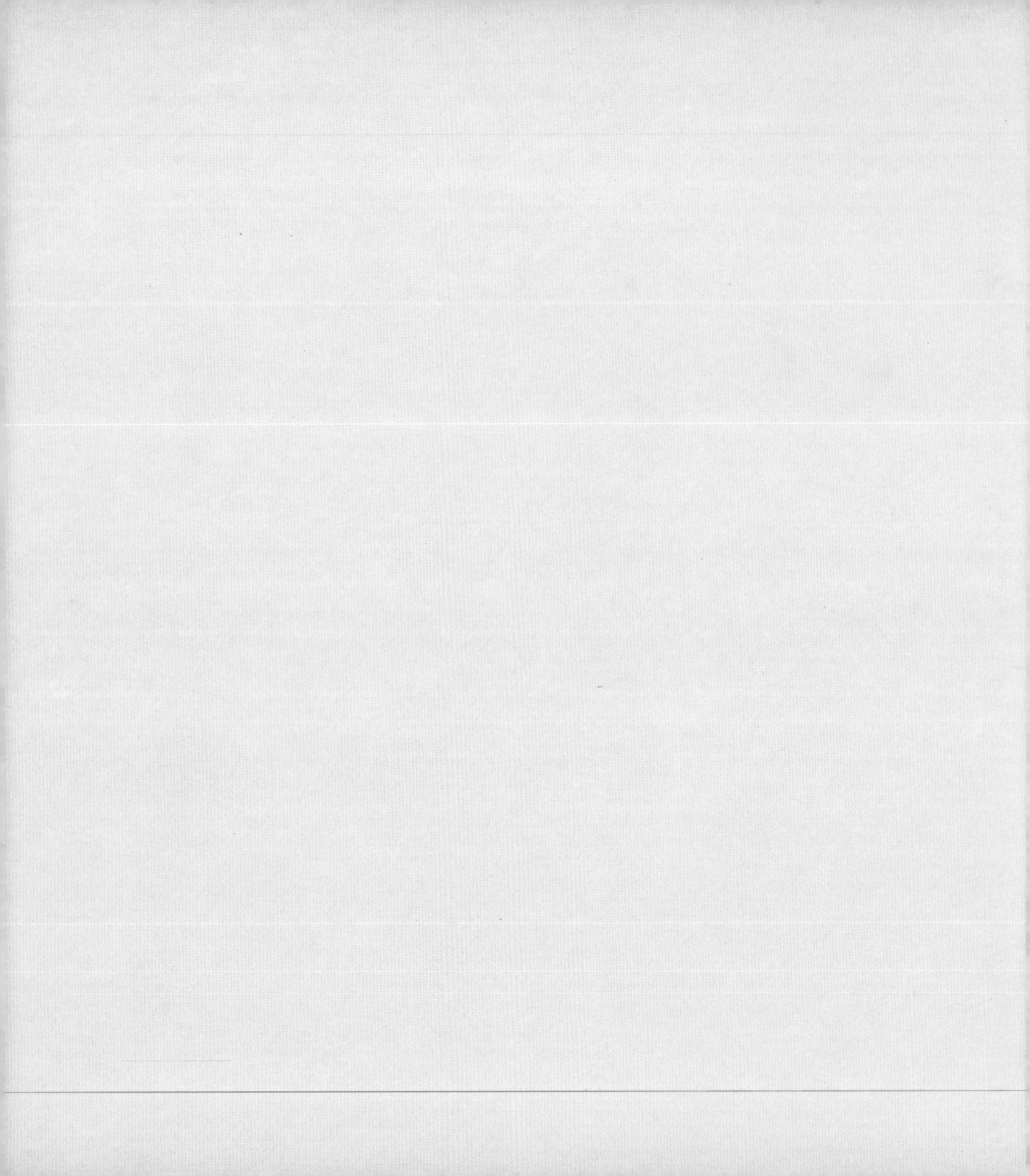